In
Dad's
Day

Acknowledgments

Executive Editor: Diane Sharpe
Supervising Editor: Stephanie Muller
Design Manager: Sharon Golden
Page Design: Simon Balley Design Associates
Photography: Barnaby's Picture Library: pages 20, 22 (left), 26; Gordon Bussey: page 7; Sally and Richard Greenhill: page 16; Hulton Deutsch: page 11 (left); Image Select: page 13 (top); Last Resort Picture Library: cover (middle right), pages 9 (bottom), 19, 22 (right); Trustees of the National Cycle Museum, Lincoln: cover (top right), page 11 (right); Popperfoto: page 14; Tony Stone Worldwide: pages 24-25; Topham Picture Source: cover (bottom), pages 9 (top), 13 (bottom).

Library of Congress Cataloging-In-Publication Data

Humphrey, Paul, 1952-
    In Dad's day/Paul Humphrey; illustrated by Katy Sleight.
      p.   cm. — (Read all about it. Social studies. Level A)
      Summary: In briefly captioned drawings and photographs, a father tells his son and daughter what things were like when he was young.
    ISBN 0-8114-5731-1 Hardcover
    ISBN 0-8114-3718-3 Softcover
    [1. Fathers — Fiction.]   I. Sleight, Katy, ill.   II. Title.   III. Series: Read all about it (Austin, Tex.).   Social studies.   Level A.
PZ7.H8973Ian   1995
[E]—dc20

94-28578
CIP
AC

2 3 4 5 6 7 8 9 0 PO 00 99 98 97 96 95 94

In Dad's Day

Paul Humphrey

Illustrated by
Katy Sleight

STECK-VAUGHN
COMPANY
ELEMENTARY • SECONDARY • ADULT • LIBRARY

4

I did many things.
Now, let me think.

Yes, but the pictures on our TV were only black and white.

My toys looked like this. My favorite
was my train set.

Yes, my bike looked like this.
It was called a chopper.

When I was young, cars looked like this. I had to help clean my dad's car.

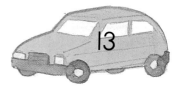

13

When I was young, I watched TV to see the first man walk on the Moon.

14

When I was a teenager, we wore clothes like these.

16

I played my records.

Sometimes I went to a disco.

21

I listened to pop music
on my transistor radio.

When I was a teenager, I saw the
first Concorde fly above.

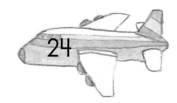

24

When I was 18, I had a motorcycle.

27

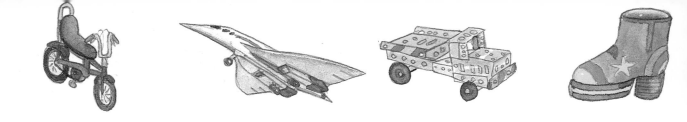

When you are a dad, you can tell your children about all the things you did when you were young.

Yes, I'll have so much to tell them.

29

Which of the things on this page belong to Dad's time, and which belong to today?

Index